D1172801

Balfour and Meriwether

—in—

The

Incident

— of the —

Harrowmoor Dogs

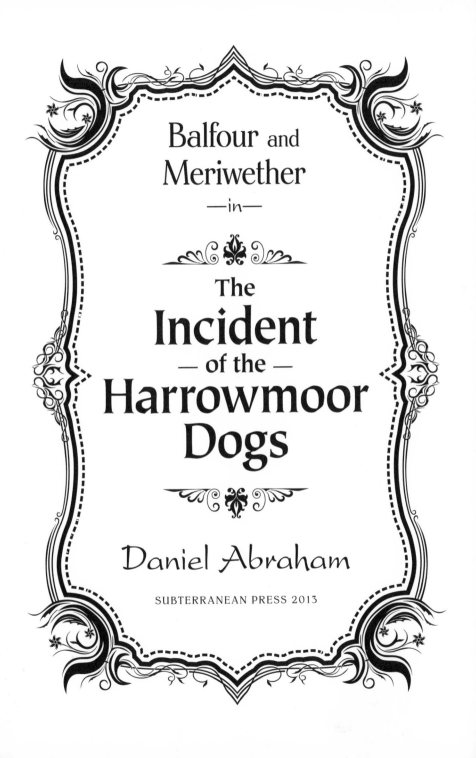

Balfour and
Meriwether

—in—

The
Incident
— of the —
**Harrowmoor
Dogs**

Daniel Abraham

SUBTERRANEAN PRESS 2013

First Edition

ISBN
978-1-59606-576-5

Subterranean Press
PO Box 190106
Burton, MI 48519

subterraneanpress.com

LONDON IN SPRINGTIME can be a thing of unsurpassed beauty. The air this morning was crisp as a new-plucked apple, and as I sit here in the gardens waiting for my tea, the sun is as warm as an old friend. From the house, I hear the sounds of the new wireless that Julius and Ethel brought me when last they had returned from India, and a not a moment ago, a group of young men came racing down the street on bicycles, voices raised in laughter and the bluff tones peculiar to masculine companionship. On days such as this, the world seems a wholesome place. And so it is, in part. But only in part.

Nature in her vastness and variety produces both the straight branch and the gnarled, the noble lion and the innocent lamb and the monstrous serpent. I know only too well that the young men of England, fresh of face and broad of shoulder, share the Earth with other beings equally the products of Nature but informed less by Christ than by His eternal enemy. And in all my years of work with Mr. Balfour, and despite my unshakable faith in him, there remains one secret to which I alone am privy...

— From the Last Notebook of Mr. Meriwether, 1920

CHAPTER ONE:

The Inverted Man

IT WAS THE TWENTY-EIGHTH of April, 188- and a day of warmth, beauty, and commerce in the crowded streets of London, but Lord Carmichael's features had a distinctly wintery aspect. He stood by the front window of the King Street flat, scowling down at the cobbled streets. The snifter of brandy in his left hand was all but forgotten. Behind his back, Meriwether caught Balfour's gaze and lifted his eyebrows. Balfour stroked his broad mustache and cleared his throat. The sound was very nearly an apology. For a long moment, it seemed Lord Carmichael had not so much as heard it, but then he heaved a great sigh and turned back to the men.

The flat itself was in a state of utter disarray. The remains of the breakfast sat beside the empty fire grate, and the body of a freshly slaughtered pig lay stretched out across the carpeted floor, its flesh marked out in squares by lines of lampblack and a variety of knives protruding from it, one in each square. Meriwether's silver flute perched upon the mantle in a nest of musical notation, and a half-translated treatise on the effects of certain new world plant extracts upon human memory sat abandoned on the desk. Lord Carmichael's eyes lifted to the two agents of the Queen as he stepped over the porcine corpse and took his seat.

"I'm afraid we have need of you, boys," Lord Carmichael said. "Daniel Winters is missing."

"Surely not an uncommon occurrence," Meriwether said, affecting a lightness of tone. "My understanding was that our friend Winters has quite the reputation for losing himself in the fleshpots of the empire between missions. I would have expected him to have some difficulty finding him*self*, most mornings."

"He wasn't between missions," Lord Carmichael said. "He was engaged in an enquiry."

"Queen's business?" Balfour said.

"Indirectly. It was a blue rose affair."

Balfour sat forward, thick fists under his chin and a flinty look in his eyes. Among all the concerns and intrigues that Lord Carmichael had the managing of, the blue rose affairs were the least palatable not from any moral or ethical failure—Balfour and Meriwether understood the near-Jesuitical deformations of ethics and honor that the defense of the Empire could require—but rather because they were so often lacking in the rigor they both cultivated.

When a housewife in Bath woke screaming that a fairy had warned her of a threat against the Queen, it was a blue rose affair. When a young artist lost his mind and slaughtered prostitutes, painting in their blood to open a demonic gate, it was a blue rose affair. When a professor of economics was tortured to the edge of madness by dreams of an ancient and sleeping god turning foul and malefic eyes upon the human world, it was a blue rose affair. And so almost without fail, they were wastes of time and effort, ending in confirmations of hysteria that posed no threat and offered no benefit to anyone sane. Meriwether took his seat, propping his heels on the dead pig. As if in response, a bit of trapped gas escaped the hog like a sigh.

"I am surprised Winters would involve himself in such a thing," Meriwether said. "He always struck me as being more the sort of man that concerned himself with fisticuffs, opium, and women of negotiable virtue. I have a hard time imagining him wading through the ectoplasmic fantasies of underemployed ladies after greater mystical truths."

"Spiritualist twaddle," Balfour said.

"It was as a favor to me," Lord Carmichael said. "Tell me, gentlemen. What do you know of Michael Caster?"

"The explorer?" Balfour asked, his eyes narrowing.

"The very one," Lord Carmichael said.

"We know what everyone would, I suppose," Meriwether said. "He was a great hero against the Zulu under Lord Chelmsford, and after his victories in Africa spent some years with the Royal Society. I have his account of seeking the roots of the Prester John and his monograph on the source of the Nile. He also put out several volumes of quite decent poetry. Is he involved in this too?"

"A year ago, Caster had something of a nervous fit. Very little was made of it in the press, thank God. He retired to Harrowmoor Sanitarium for the rest cure, and he's been there ever since. Last month, he submitted a collection of sonnets for publication. Some references in them seemed to imply a greater knowledge of certain sensitive projects than Caster could be expected to possess. Winters was back from the Russias and I thought I could keep him sober for a few days more if he went to enquire. He left for Harrowmoor at the beginning of the month. His last report, such as it is, arrived nine days ago."

Lord Carmichael pulled a folded scrap of paper from his pocket and held it out. Balfour stretched out a thick-fingered hand and plucked it away. The paper hissed as he unfolded it. His gaze shot along the lines of crabbed script and inkblots. His eyes widened.

"Delirium tremens?" the thick man suggested, handing the letter across to Meriwether.

"Perhaps," Lord Carmichael said and sipped his brandy. "I sent to him at once. There has been no reply, and the couriers I have commissioned since cannot find him. I need you boys to pop over to Harrowmoor and see what there is to be seen."

"A buried and bestial England," Meriwether said. "A prettier turn of phrase than I expect from our constitutionally discontented Winters. I don't imagine you have any thoughts what it might signify?"

"I'm afraid I can't say."

Balfour let out a grunt. Meriwether, agreeing, handed back the letter. "There's more than one way to unpack that answer, old friend."

"There are some aspects of this I'm not at liberty to discuss, even with you," Lord Carmichael said. "Just find what's happened to Winters and bring him back if you can. And also, for the love of Christ, why *is* there a pig carcass on your floor?"

❧

IT TOOK the better part of the afternoon to bring their affairs in London into a condition that they might be safely let stand for a fortnight. When near twilight, Balfour and Meriwether stepped out to the street, Lord Carmichael's carriage awaited them. Meriwether's paired revolvers were obscured by the volume of his greatcoat, and Balfour's brace of knives were little more than irregular bumps in his vest, invisible to all but his tailor. The men nodded to the driver, took their places within the carriage. They lurched into the street to the rough music of hooves, wheels, and cobblestones. Balfour stared out the window as Meriwether tapped a gentle fingertip tattoo against his own knees. The sense of dread between them would have been invisible to any other man, but they were more than cognizant of it.

"Winters is a cad with the style of a bawdy house and the manners of a bulldog," Meriwether said. "I wouldn't give him a penny I needed repaid."

"Competent, though," Balfour muttered.

"One of the best. I'm afraid we may find more at the end of this than too much vice and too little restraint."

"Know when we get there," Balfour said, but his manner was agreement enough.

At the station, they strode past the crowded plaforms of London and stepped into the private car arranged for their use. Meriwether lit a pipe against the stink of coal smoke and oil, and with the fading rays of the sunset, the train pulled out from the station and proceeded into darkness.

Harrowmoor stood on a low cliff at the edge of the sea. It boasted fewer than three hundred souls in the town itself, and perhaps as many again eking out rough lives among the low, treeless hills. The landscape seemed to flow out behind the town itself like an unending shawl draped on the shoulders of the buildings as they stared out at the cold sea. The train station was illuminated by a single lantern in the hand of a venerable stationmaster, and Balfour and Meriwether stepped down from their car into the deep and moonlit night with a sense of profound isolation. In London, gentlemen would still be drinking and smoking cigars in their clubs, but Harrowmoor lived by a different clock. The distance between the two habitations of humanity was as profound as if the pair had stepped onto the coldly shining moon. The frost-haired stationmaster ambled to them, his skin colorless in his lamp's dim light. His eyes were wide-set, and even when he smiled, the thick, sluggish lips had something of the fish in their aspect.

"Gentlemen," he said, bobbing his head. "I hope the trip was pleasant."

"Quite," Meriwether said. "And our thanks to you, my friend, for staying up to meet us."

"Always do," the stationmaster said. "Most nights, we don't see anyone on the last train, but those times we do, it's best that someone meets them. Wouldn't want strangers getting lost. Not at night. You're for the sanitarium, yes?"

"Come to visit, yes," Meriwether said.

"Of course, of course," the old man said, turning toward the street. "You two gentlemen don't have the consumption. I've seen them come and I've seen them go, and I can tell. Better than the nurses, I am. Only takes a look, and I can say whether a man's too far gone. No mysteries left for me." He let out a rasping chuckle like a rusted clockwork.

"I understand our cousin preceded us," Meriwether said, trotting to keep pace. "Perhaps you might have met him as well?"

"If they come by train, I see them."

"Young man," Balfour said. "Brown hair, pale eyes. Scar across the back of his left hand."

The stationmaster shook his head. "Nonesuch by land. Might have come by water, though. Some do."

The street beyond the train station was narrow and black. The stars overhead shed too little light, and rather than dispelling the shadows, the ruddy lantern made them seem deeper. A squat building stood on the near corner, the light and scent and soft mutter of voices marking it as a public house. A sign hung before it was rendered illegible by the darkness.

"Here's the Black Hound, gentlemen. Best lodging in Harrowmoor, the sanitarium notwithstanding," the station-master said with a wheezing chuckle. Meriwether turned back. The lit carriage windows of the train sixty feet away shone brighter than the slivered moon.

"It seems a short enough walk to make unchaperoned," he said.

"Like it does, sir," the stationmaster said. "But men get turned around in the dark sometimes, and we're not far from the moorland. Will-o-the-wisps sometimes too. Lead men where they oughtn't be, and that's not good. Safer this way is all. Safer." He nodded to himself as if impressed by his own wisdom.

Meriwether drew a coin from his pocket and pressed it into the old man's palm. The fishy eyes went wide when they caught the metal's color.

"My thanks," Meriwether said. "Really, you've been more than kind. I was wondering if you might know something of the man we've come to see."

"Kind of you, sir, but I haven't seen your cousin—"

"Not him," Meriwether said. "We've come to interview a famous explorer and war hero. His name is Michael Caster."

The stationmaster's face shifted, deforming into a comic mask of disgust. His scowl was so profound, the corner of his mouth seemed to droop almost past the line of his jaw.

"That one? Yes, I saw him when he came through. Would have been about a year ago now. Strong fellow. Wide across the shoulders. Smoked them black Turkish cigars. Oh, yes, I remember that one."

"We've not met him," Meriwether said. "Not yet. Anything you could tell us that would be of use would be appreciated."

The stationmaster glanced at the coin in his hand, then slid it into his pocket with a sigh. "We see a fair number come up to the sanitarium. Consumption. Nerves. Women with hysteria or the cancer. Men with them sicknesses they catch from women on the continent. All sorts, and I ain't one to judge. Not the sort of man I am, but that Mr. Caster of yours? I met his train too, and I'll tell you this for certain. What's wrong with him can't be fixed."

The pub's mistress was a thick-featured and sullen woman who took as little time as possible in greeting them, seeing them fed bowls of roasted chicken and overcooked beans, and sending them off to their room. Meriwether's gentle and probing questions concerning Winters could as well have been asked to a stone. The accommodations were close and rusticated, with a single bed and rushes on the floor like something from Chaucer. A gentle sobbing sound passed through the thin walls from an adjacent room, and the awareness that their privacy was compromised brought their conversation down to whispers as they took turns making their ablutions at the small basin.

"Charming place."

"It isn't the last word in luxury or hygiene, that's true, but you must agree is has its own distinctive style. The combination of crushing poverty and gleeful judgment of others speaks of rural England at its most morally supine. A perfect example of its species, I'd say. The very epitome of things best left uncelebrated."

Balfour grunted, pulling off his boot, then drew the hidden blade from its seam. The candlelight danced along the well-oiled steel, and the mustached man returned it to its sheath with a sense of satisfaction. Meriwether laid his own weapons out on the bed cover, deftly disassembling and reassembling the revolvers as they spoke.

"Winters and Caster," Balfour murmured.

"The former must have taken lodging somewhere, and is, after all, the subject of our proximate investigation. It is even possible that his disappearance bears less on this present enquiry than on some other business with roots sunk half around the globe and which only happened to bloom here and now."

"Can find Caster, though."

"It is a point in his favor that Michael Caster has fallen where there is light," Meriwether said. "And if Winters did interview the man, it's more than possible that Caster may know something of what preceded the disappearance. So which scent do we follow? The hunter Winters or the man Caster whom he hunted?"

Balfour hung his vest on the back of a chair and began pulling his blades one by one, testing each edge as he did. In his shirtsleeves, his body seemed a solid knot of muscle. Meriwether finished reassembling his pistols and slid them back into their paired holsters. There was not so much as a drop of oil to mar the bedding where he had worked.

"Both," Balfour said.

"I had drawn the same conclusion. I will repair to the sanitarium in the morning if you like and leave you the task of tracking down word of Winters here in the town."

"No difference to me," Balfour said.

"You are an eminently agreeable man," Meriwether said, and both men smiled at the joke. "Is there anything in this present matter on which you do have a preference?"

"First watch," Balfour said, "and the side against the wall."

THE SANITARIUM stood half a mile out from the town, but the road to it was solid and well-maintained. The white walls rose above the bare landscape like the bones of the earth itself. Seagulls wheeled in the white sky, calling mindlessly to one another. To the east, the sea stretched grey and uneasy to the horizon, to the west, the moor rolled, hill after low, scrub-choked hill, and Meriwether would have been hard pressed to say whether land or sea bore the more forbidding aspect. Only the scattering of trees that rose above the sanitarium walls hinted at some other world within, a secret garden inaccessible as Eden denied. The nurse who greeted him stood half a head below him. Her uniform was a blinding white that was meant, he felt sure, to indicate purity and health, but left Meriwether thinking in vague and unpleasant ways of sterilization.

The interior of the sanitarium surrounded a courtyard. Half a dozen men sat on chairs beneath the boughs of stunted oaks. The youngest of the men looked hardly more than a boy, his skin the color of fresh-turned clay. The oldest of them, his hair reduced to wisps and his skin a map of cavernous wrinkles, had half-closed eyes and brown lower teeth exposed by his gaping jaw. If it was Eden, it was one peopled by the lepers hoping for the Savior's kind hand. Meriwether felt the growing certainty that few of the sanitarium's patients were destined to leave.

The chief physician's office looked out over the courtyard, but was not so high as to see over the sanitarium's outer wall. The effect was of a beautiful and well-tended world that stopped suddenly. Glassed cabinets displayed a variety of medical equipment, a menagerie of steel and vulcanized rubber. The man himself was thin as a weed with dishwater blond hair slicked back over protruding ears. He stepped from his desk with his hand extended.

"Mr. Meriwether! Come in, come in," he said in a quacking American accent. "Any friend of Lord Carmichael is welcome here. Take a chair. Can I offer you a cup of tea?"

"I appreciate the offer, but..."

"All right. Your choice." The physician dropped back into his seat with a grin, like a child at Christmas.

Meriwether crossed his legs. "I've come to enquire about a patient of yours. Michael Caster."

"Yes, of course. Hard one. Nervous excess. Aberrant, self-destructive behavior. It was his uncle who got him here, bless the man. Became concerned that Michael would do himself permanent harm. He's been with us for almost a year now."

"Self-destructive behavior?" Meriwether prompted.

"Very much so," the physician said. "Yes, indeed, very much so."

When it became clear that no further details would be forthcoming, Meriwether changed tacks. "Has his condition improved since his arrival?"

The physician leaned forward, his fingertips pressed to his bloodless lips. "Truth to tell, I can't say he has. He's changed plenty. When he first came, he was angry all the time. Lashing out. We had to sedate him for most of June, but once that course was complete, the violence of his outbursts lessened. He's calmer now, but with nightmares five, six times a week. And his underlying condition… No, sir, I'd love to tell you he's getting better, but I'd be lying."

"I understand he has been publishing poetry?"

"Yes, I've allowed him—encouraged him, even—to express himself through his work. It seems to give him some relief, but as a long-term therapy, it isn't having the effect I'd hoped. He works, and some of his compositions are quite memorable, but there's a darkness in them that only seems to be growing. His outward demeanor is pleasant enough, but I can't say we've plumbed the depths of this. Not at all."

"His long-term prospects are bleak, then?"

"Wouldn't say that," the physician said. "We have a lot of tools in our chest we haven't pulled out yet. Aversion, chemical therapies. There's some fascinating work with direct manipulation of the living brain being done back in Ohio that holds promise. He's a brilliant young man, and we're a long way from giving up on him."

"May I meet with him?"

"Of course," the physician said. "I think he'd like that. He was very pleased when that last fellow came. Winters?"

"Yes," Meriwether said, rising to his feet. As they stepped toward the doorway, he paused. The physician looked back at him, inquiry in his expression. "Does Mr. Caster do his work in his room?"

"The writing you mean? He does."

"Might I have a moment in there alone before our meeting? I've found I can learn a great deal about a man by the way he lives and works."

The physician blinked like an owl, then shrugged. "Can't see any reason not to. If you find something that could give me some insight into the fella, you'll pass it on." It was phrased almost as a request. Meriwether had the sense that the chief physician was unaccustomed to having his will questioned.

"Of course," Meriwether said. "Lead on, and we will find what can be found."

❧

THE ROOM was small and neatly kept. White plaster walls rose above the simple bed and small working desk. Three leather-bound notebooks rested beside a stub of pencil, charcoal, and a rubber eraser. The sheets were folded with precision, and the chair at the desk stood neatly in its place. Meriwether held out both his arms, fingertips just brushing the opposing walls. The space itself reminded him of a monk's cell, peaceful and clean and utterly divorced from the world. He ran his hands along the bedclothes, but no secret items disclosed themselves. The flat pillow held nothing but a few handfuls of limp feathers. Sharpened iron bars bloomed from the window-sill, preventing birds from roosting and inhabitants from leaving with equal facility. The chief physician haunted the doorway, bouncing slightly on the balls of his feet, as if in anticipation of some discovery, some new chink in his patient's psychic armor.

Meriwether picked up the notebooks, thumbing through the pages slowly, carefully. The script within was legible and controlled. Even on those pages, and there were several, where the author had been struggling with the scansion of some particular phrase, it was done with the precision and regularity of a draughtsman. In among the poems and notes, there were also sketches rendered in pencil and coal. Most had the precision and beauty of anatomical studies: a tree standing along the side of a page with the texture of bark and leaf made clear, the study of a beetle in all three planes, and even the room in which Meriwether now stood as seen from the bed. They were technically admirable and displayed a profound if analytical sensitivity, and Meriwether expected much the same of the poems until he reached the third notebook. Here, the images became stranger and more phantas-magorical. Strange beasts, half hound and half insect, stared out from the pages, vicious teeth snapping. And then another image, a single sketch which stood out from the others.

It was of a young man in his shirtsleeves, fair-haired with the faintest of smiles pulling at the soft charcoal lips. The figure wore trousers high on his waist and rested on one hand as through he were leaning against a wall. The masculine gray eyes were fixed upon the viewer, and Meriwether felt his eyebrows rise and his heart step up its pace in surprise. And indeed shock. The man depicted was unfamiliar, but his pose and intent could not be mistaken. He was powerfully beautiful, the apotheosis of the masculine animal. All he knew of Michael Caster came into a sudden new perspective.

"Ah, guests then," an unfamiliar voice said. "Please don't wait for my permission. Make yourselves at home."

Michael Caster was the human embodiment of his room. Light brown hair cut neatly and close to the neck. His build was trim and athletic, and the rage at their invasion of his privacy hardly showed in his sky blue eyes. His shirt was the same white as the nurses' uniforms, but on him, it spoke more of an unpainted canvas awaiting the artist's stroke. His trousers were dark and ill-fitting. They were the sort that the other patients wore, likely all laundered together and returned afterward to whomever was in need. A uniform for the damned. He seemed too young to have served in the Zulu wars, but when Meriwether looked closely, the signs were there. The first dusting of gray at his temple, the places where his skin though still unmarked would show one day a permanent crease. Meriwether put down the notebook.

"Now Michael," the physician began, "you know that—"

"I apologize," Meriwether said. "The intrusion was at my request. I'm afraid I may have let your status as a patient distract me from the constraints of courtesy. The fault is mine."

Caster lifted his chin as if hearing an unfamiliar sound. Something between amusement and distrust plucked at his lips.

"Mr. Meriwether's come to speak with you, Michael."

"If you don't mind, of course," Meriwether said.

"Anything to shake up the monotony, I suppose," he said carefully. "I will have to check with my social secretary, but I believe I was slated to be here the whole day. I get out so rarely, you know."

Meriwether turned to the chief physician with a polite smile. "Thank you very much for all your help in this. Lord Carmichael will be very pleased."

The dismissal was so polite that for a moment the physician didn't understand it had been delivered. His eyes widened for a moment and then a pale smile drew back his lips. He began to speak, stopped, nodded to both men and stepped away holding his head high. Caster chuckled low in his throat.

"He won't thank you for that," Caster said. "The good doctor is unaccustomed to being excluded."

"It will be good practice for him, then," Meriwether said, then took a breath and plunged at once to the vulnerable point. "I was led to understand that you came to the sanitarium after a fit of nerves. That isn't true, is it?"

"No." Caster crossed his arms. His gaze shifted onto the blankness of the wall.

"You are inverted. A homosexual."

"I…am." The man's voice moved slowly, carefully, picking its way among the syllables as if they might bite. "Not that I see it is any of your concern."

"It is what brought you here, however?"

"It was," Caster said. He held his body square as a man before the firing squad. "I was involved with a younger man. It was unwise and rash, but I was very much in love. His father discovered us, and my uncle, soul of Christian charity that he is, arranged for my indefinite incarceration here rather than commending me to the law. If you have some judgment or comment you'd like to share about that, I cannot prevent you."

"It's no concern of mine," Meriwether said. "I've come looking for Daniel Winters. He's gone missing."

Caster's gaze returned, his eyes flashing with concern. "God. Missing? How long?"

Meriwether pulled out the desk chair and sat, his fingers wrapping his knee.

"We had word from him two weeks ago, but it wasn't particularly coherent. Since then, nothing."

"He's gone to them," Caster said.

"Gone to whom?"

"The dogs. The ones in my dream," Caster said. Then caught himself and shook his head, "And here you might not have thought I was mad."

"Perhaps it would be best if we began at the beginning," Meriwether said.

"The whole sordid tale?" Caster asked, stepping forward to lean against the foot of the bed. Meriwether felt himself smile almost against his will.

"Perhaps an abridgment. What did you and Mr. Winters discuss? What are the dreams you speak of, Mr. Caster, and when did they begin?"

Caster sat on the bed's edge, collecting his thoughts for a moment.

"I am not a superstitious man. I don't believe in things without some evidence to support them. When I tell you that I have always been led by my dreams, I hope you will understand it is because my dreams have been a curiously reliable guide. In Africa, I knew of the coming attacks days before they transpired. Sometimes I would even know the number of the enemy, the direction from which they would come, and the time the assault would begin. I'm not a fool. I never relied on the dreams being accurate. I only prepared in case they were, and more often than not, it was good that I had. I suspect that many of the men in my mother's family suffered the same effects. Something in the blood, I suppose. I became used to them. A sort of useful party trick, and nothing more. And then, I came to Harrowmoor.

"From my first night here, I have been plagued by nightmares. They are not always identical, but in some details, they remain consistent. Always, I am in a barn near an abandoned farmhouse. It is always twilight, the sunlight failing around me. And there is something like a well. An ancient stone shaft into the earth with walls made from stones like those of a henge, only sunk deep into the earth rather than resting upon it. I know, in the dream, that the barn was built around the well, that humanity discovered this and thought nothing more of it than a convenient place to cool milk and meat. My mind descends into the darkness. There is a world down there. Lightless, but not unpeopled. Vast cities and warrens of passages too narrow and close for the human form. It is as if a great empire had flourished beneath the earth. Passages lead not only throughout England, but under the seas to strange and foreign lands. And deeper too, leading to places where the cooling air grows hot again, and lichens and fungi feed upon the sulfurous warmth with a sluggish awareness that is almost like animal life. I feel this vastness more than see it. I experience it as you might know the state of your own body. Great beasts sleep there, and strange intelligences battle in lightless subterranean wars. I have seen things that no waking eye has ever seen. Parasite worms that dig into the living flesh of their enemies and swallow up the brains, then use the corpse as a mechanism, riding it as you or I might sit a horse. Toothed grubs that chew their mindless way through basalt and brimstone, weakening the foundations of the world itself. And the dogs. Always and without fail, the dogs."

Caster's face grew drawn, his cheeks seeming to sink into his face, his eyes darkening and becoming hollow. Absently, he rubbed his fingers together with a sound like paper sliding against paper.

"I call them that, but they have other names for themselves. They are no larger than wolves, but they possess minds of great complexity and insight and terrible, vicious purpose. Once, I believe the great underground empire may have had a thousand species that flourished in that uncanny darkness. A world below the world, if you can imagine it. It is a second, dark and cthonic world warmed from below as we are warmed from above, our shadow and our twin. Most of its inhabitants have been consumed or slaughtered, and those that remain do so because they are of use to the dogs. In the dreams, I am among them, and they know me. They can smell the traces of my dreams, and they try to follow me back. I know that if I lead them to the surface of the world, they will find me. Here, in this room, Mr. Meriwether, they will find me. And my life would be forfeit. And so I flee deeper and deeper into the underground, and the dogs follow, howling."

"Your drawings," Meriwether said. "They are of these dogs?"

"Mr. Winters asked the same thing. Yes. Those are the beasts from my dreams."

"And they are what brought him to you? I understood there was a poem."

"I have a friend in London who keeps a little salon. He collects people he finds interesting. Poets, artists, men of science and politics. It is more innocent than it sounds. He puts together a small broadsheet when it amuses him to do so and distributes it among his circle. He and I exchanged letters for a time. I sent him something I had written that mentioned the underground empire. I didn't know anyone else had seen it until your Mr. Winters appeared one day and asked about it. What had inspired it, what I knew, and how I knew it."

"And you said?"

"What I have told you, more or less. He asked for specifics of the farmhouse. The barn. I guessed that he intended to seek out the places from my dreams as if they were real. I warned him against it, and I thought at the time I had persuaded him. But perhaps not. He's found it, then? He's gone down?"

Meriwether leaned forward.

"We don't know," he said. "He has vanished, and we have come to find what we can to explain it. Knowing Mr. Winters as I do, he may have found a brewery whose wares he particularly enjoyed or a woman with a particularly fetching smile."

"But you doubt it," Caster said. "Don't you?"

"My companion is looking for him now. I have the greatest faith that whatever can be found out will be."

Caster shook his head. "Don't let him go underground. If the trail leads there, let it go. You'll have lost one man, but better that than two. Or three, I suppose."

"Mr. Balfour and I have faced many dangers," Meriwether said. "I have no doubt—"

"Nor have I, sir," Caster said. His voice was hard as stone. "You've come seeking what I know? I know that very little which falls into that dark pit returns again to the light."

A variety of witticisms presented themselves to Meriwether's tongue, but he spoke none of them. Caster's expression was so serious and bleak that to treat his concerns lightly would have been rude. Instead, he stood. A pigeon fluttered close to the window and then away, covering Caster's face for a moment with the shadow of its wings.

"Thank you for your time and attention, Mr. Caster," Meriwether said. "I think perhaps I should seek out my companion and apprise him of your advice."

Caster's smile was thin and haunted. "I think you should run, Mr. Meriwether. But before you do, may I ask you a question? As a man of the world?"

"You may."

"You divined the reason for my interment here. They have discussed a great number of treatments for me. Most recently, they have considered unmanning me surgically and giving me a course of forced sedation that would last the rest of my life, however long that might be."

Meriwether locked his hands behind him. "I have heard some such discussion, yes. But you said you had a question. That was a series of statements."

Caster nodded. "I did not ask to be what I am, nor did I choose it. As a man of the world, do you consider my inversion a disease to be cured?"

"No," Meriwether said at once. "I am a servant of crown and church, and I take my guidance from them. Homosexuality is no disease. It is a sin and an abomination."

Pain flickered in Caster's visage, and then a careful smile. How many years, Meriwether wondered, had the man practiced the art of appearing not to care?

"I am as God made me," Caster said.

"I see no contradiction," Meriwether said. "God makes many abominable things, and I am in no position to condemn His choices. But now, sir, you must excuse me. I have other monstrosities to attend to."

CHAPTER TWO:

Voices From the Deep

AFTER LEAVING MERIWETHER'S COMPANY in the morning, Balfour began with a leisurely walk through the town. His first impulse in times like these was toward violence and threats, and so it was only through an act of will that he restrained himself from direct action. Before the campaign could begin in earnest, it was best to know the battlefield. He strode through the dark streets with his nearest approximation of joviality, his eyes shifting constantly from face to face, from building to building, without seeking any one thing in particular. And so he allowed himself the luxury of building a sense of Harrowmoor Town, and with it a better idea of where his efforts might be properly placed.

In daylight, some part of the town's grim aspect disappeared, but only some. The clay of the earth itself held a grayness that seemed to have worked into the skin of the townsmen. The children laughed and played in the streets just as they did in any such place, but their chants and whistles had a cruel undertone. The horses that pulled the carts down the streets had an empty exhaustion in their eyes that recalled men too long in battle who had become inured to the trauma of their surroundings. Soul-dead. There were neither cats nor dogs anywhere in evidence. Balfour's own presence elicited neither curiosity nor remark. The trade of the sanitarium, he supposed, would bring a steady stream of odd and grieving humanity to Harrowmoor. He might have been a physician come to consult about a difficult patient or a man with a consumptive wife dying by gasps upon the far hill. The townsmen would be accustomed to strangers passing through. Perhaps so much so as to be blinded to them.

As he stepped into the small market square with its half dozen rickety stalls and sun-bleached awnings, he found himself wondering how many men had died in the sanitarium, and whether the concentration of so much suffering and death might somehow have poisoned the land itself. Or possibly the moorland had always carried a sense of doom and disquiet, and so become the natural home of the hopeless and dying.

He shook himself, trying to shrug off the malaise that threatened to overcome him as well. He hadn't come to ruminate upon the effects of mortality on the landscape. He was here to find Winters, or if not the man, at least his track. He scanned the stalls and streets, willing himself to see them not only as he did, but as his prey might have. A white-haired crone stood at a stall, a basket of eggs before her. At another, a thin man with a tremor in his hands shooed flies away from a display if disreputable-looking meat pies. Two young toughs leaned against the wall at the mouth of a bright alley hardly less dignified than the street it opened upon. The boys were caught between leering at a young woman walk-ing down the sidewalk and embarrassment at their own lust.

"If I were Winters…" Balfour said to himself. Then he quirked a smile. The question was not only what Winters would have done, but who would have noticed him doing it. For that, the solution was obvious. He stroked his mustache in satisfaction and trundled across to the two young men. The boys scowled at him and pretended to look away until his focus and intent were impossible to ignore.

"You there," he said. "I'm looking for a man was here a few weeks back."

The taller of the two youths had lank, dark hair and a rot-brown front tooth. His shorter companion was still taller than Balfour with sand-colored hair and a weak attempt at a beard.

"Lots of men come through," Rot-tooth shrugged. "Don't matter to us."

Unfortunate Beard pulled a worn work knife from his boot and began cleaning his fingernails with it. Balfour felt a wave of pleasure as he plucked it from the boy's unprac-ticed hands. Unfortunate Beard's eyes narrowed in anger until Balfour shifted his vest, displaying his brace of knives, and then they went wide.

"This would have been a gentleman in his thirties. Dark hair, light eyes. Handsome and a bit full of himself. Scar across the back of his hand. Would have made propositions to any girl in town whose heels looked even slightly rounded. Now, my guess is you boys are more aware than anyone else what men are talking to which girls. And so I think you know who I'm speaking of. Yes?"

The two looked at each other. Their uncertainty spoke volumes.

"What's he to you?" Rot-tooth asked. Balfour hardly had to consider which lie to tell.

"He's a friend of my wife's," he said coldly, and let the knives and implications speak for themselves. It took little time for the boys to imagine bloody vengeance taken upon their imagined sexual rival. As though they were anywhere near Winters' league.

"Right, then. We've seen him. Stayed in the Black Dog for a week, then started out for the moors."

"The moors?"

"That's right. Walked all over them, night and day. Probably got caught in a bog."

"Last I heard," Unfortunate Beard said, "he was staying at the old Phillips place. Farmhouse halfway to Fenton. No one's lived there since old man Phillips died of the cancer and his daughters lit out for the colonies."

Balfour smiled and handed back the worn knife, handle first. Unfortunate Beard took it.

"Don't suppose you fine gents could give me directions," Balfour rumbled, his voice a graveled mixture of pleasure and the threat of violence. "And then see to it that no one mentions to our mutual friend that anyone's looking for him."

Half an hour's time later, and still well before lunch, Balfour had an egg sandwich in one pocket, a bottle of beer in the other, and clear directions out through the moorland to the farmhouse where Winters had last been known to abide. He walked with a bit of a spring in his step despite the treeless, grim surroundings, buoyed up by the predictability of jealous young men and randy old ones. Between Winters' penchant for flirtation and the local adolescents' resentment of it, Balfour had the thread to walk this unwalled labyrinth.

The sun rose high in the great pale bowl of the heavens, and the moor stood quietly beneath it. Low hills flowed down from the town, the land growing wetter with each new small valley. The whine of insects filled the air with mindless, tuneless song that soon dispelled Balfour's bright mood. Gorse and wild blackberry grew unchecked beside the paths, their leaves bright and forbidding. It wasn't until he paused to eat his sandwich and beer that Balfour noticed the little details that had been troubling him. The moor was rich with plants and insects, but no animals seemed to live here. No rabbits had chewed back the brush. No voles or mice fled at his approach. The sense of being utterly alone was as profound as it was uneasing.

The farmhouse, when he found it, was unmistakable both in its identity and its emptiness. Weather had stripped the doors of their paint, leaving the exposed wood to rot. The thatching of the roof sported weeds and wildflowers, and trails of black moss dripped down the walls beneath it. Balfour drew his knives, holding the blades against his wrists in case there should be anyone watching from within the derelict structure. Silent as a cat, Balfour stepped forward. Broken windows stared blindly at his progress. When he eased the door open, the stink of mildew, fungus, and rot assailed him. The soft ticking of insects in the thatch and the groan of floorboards under his weight were the only sounds as he stepped through the modest structure. The rooms were close and the walls sagged at strange and disturbing angles. His intellect told him that once a family had made their home in this place, but his imagination could not encompass the thought. The farmhouse was so profoundly ruined he could only believe it had sprung up already destroyed at the beginning of the world.

In the back room, he found what could only have been Daniel Winters' camp. A glass lantern stood on a stool, thick yellow oil in its reservoir and soot darkening its glass. A bedroll lay on the floor beside it, threads of mold already creeping across the wool. With the point of one blade, Balfour folded back the cloth, then lifted it. The holes that

pierced it were ragged. Torn, then. Not cut. The blood was
black, rotten, and copious enough to speak of a superficial
wound but not of immediate death. Whatever had taken
Winters, it had taken him here. A leather notebook still
lay under the pillow alongside a small, brutal-looking pistol. Balfour sat back on his haunches for a moment, then
turned the book with a knifepoint, inspecting it carefully
before committing his bare fingers to holding it. The writing within was the schoolboy's scrawl he'd seen on reports
from Cairo and Munich, though wider and less controlled.
Winters without a doubt. He riffled the pages quickly until
the paper went blank, and then went back to the final entries.
They were as coherent as the report to Lord Carmichael,
and perhaps less.

*Yes fiat lux and then we're buggered. Light is the only hope
against these bastards. Empires and then empires. Carmichael's
mad—don't want a gun if you can't tell the barrel from the grip,
he said, well too right. They can't get in here, or they'd have by
now. Still get the feeling the bloody things are playing with me.*

Balfour paged back. There was little that made more
sense. Partly, no doubt, was the nature of the document. Had
Winters been writing something other than prompts to his
own memory, it might have been very different indeed. On
the other hand, he'd known his letter to Lord Carmichael
had possessed a separate audience. Unless Winters had had
some reason for making his correspondence obscure, even
to those who might read it legitimately...

Balfour's head snapped up like a hound scenting a fox. His body went perfectly still, and he waited, his ears straining to recapture the thin thread of sound. It came again. Little more than a trembling of the air. Still, it had not been his imagination. Balfour tucked the notebook in his pocket and reacquired a firm grim on his knives. He moved like a shadow, his senses keen as a fresh scrape. The stink of burnt beans lingered in the still air of the kitchen. The back door stood shattered in its frame. Balfour knelt, considering the mark on the floorboards. The pale mud showed wide marks like a massive dog's paw, but lengthened at the fore with something like fingers. The sound came again, and there was no doubt this time. It was a human voice, and it was screaming.

The barn stood behind the farmhouse, its blackened timbers stinking of rot. The great door hung open. The shrieks seemed to come from beyond the structure until Balfour moved to its farther side. Then they shifted and seemed to come from the house. It was as if another landscape existed within the confines of the ruined barn, the tortured man lost somewhere much more distant than the frail walls contained. Balfour scowled and made his approach. Within, pillars of light dappled the empty spaces, shining from the holes in the church-high roof. Abandoned stalls showed where cattle had once stood. A ladder still rose up to a hayloft, dust-heavy webs empty and exhausted between the rungs. In the rear of the place, as if squatting

in the shadows, a low slab of stone with a gaping square hole four feet to a side at its center. A thick rope led from an iron ring in a stout oaken beam to the edge of the darkness, and disappeared within it. Balfour surveyed the uncomfortable mixture of shadows and light to be certain no attacker lurked to pitch him into the black well before he squatted at its mouth. The screaming was louder here, distinct and specific. And also dreadfully familiar.

"Winters?" he shouted. "Winters, is that you? Can you hear me, man?"

The screaming did not change. Balfour rubbed the back of one hand against his chin. No flicker of light shone in the darkness below, and the sunlight revealed not more than six feet of rough stone before it too failed. Balfour rose to his feet, casting eyes around the darkness.

"Hold strong, man," Balfour bellowed. "I'm coming down."

Balfour ran back to the farmhouse, retrieved the oil lantern, and lit it with a match from his own pocket. The thin, buttery light seemed too weak for the powerful darkness of the well, but there was no time to find a better torch. Reluctantly, Balfour sheathed his knives, took the lamp in one hand, and wrapped the rope around the other tightly enough to grip but not so much that he could not choose to let himself slip down. With the physical confidence of a man well-versed in violence, he set feet to stone and began lowering himself down into darkness.

The rock face before him glittered with the damp, and the soles of his shoes slipped more than once, cracking his kneecaps hard against the unforgiving stone. Cool air rose around him, carrying with it the smell of deep earth and perhaps something else: a rough and acrid stink like rancid piss. The effort of the descent made Balfour's jaw clench so firmly that his teeth creaked with the pressure. The thin flame in the lamp shuddered in the cool air around him, and the gray square of daylight grew smaller and more distant. With every yard, the ache in his arm grew until the muscles began to tremble. Any return to the world of sky and sunlight would require the use of both hands, but the thought of making this transit without the small light he carried filled him with an inexplicable dread.

The vast stones slipped seamlessly past him, defying any thought of mere human construction. No monolith so great had stood beneath the great bowl of the sky, but the mineral vastness of the earth below him seemed at once as vast as the heavens and close as a grave. Winters' ongoing shrieks did nothing to calm his nerves, but decades of study gave him the mental discipline to peg his fears at mere brusk annoyance. It seemed that the trial might go on forever, the rough hemp sliding around his elbow and across his palm until he reached the doors of hell itself, and then the shaft's end came into the sphere of light, and Balfour dropped the last few feet.

The ground beneath him was a thick clay that made soft, unpleasant sounds under his feet and pulled at his shoes. Two low tunnels led into the deep earth, lightless as dead eyes. Balfour shook his rope-scraped hand until the feeling returned to his fingers, then plucked a blade from its sheath. The steel seemed brighter than the flame that illuminated it. The tunnels, while almost ten feet across, stood little more than four feet high. To move forward, he would have to bend low and leave at least one of his flanks exposed. Balfour's mustache quivered with disgust at the tactical situation, but he chose which of the tunnels the screaming seemed to emit from and moved forward. Winters had to be close now. The screams had an exhausted quality, as a body might make when the intelligence controlling it had abdicated, a harsh and mindless sound. The stink was worse here, but he ignored it. The darkness seemed to suck away the light and give nothing in return. Balfour cursed quietly under his breath, and then called out.

"Winters! Stop making that racket. Where are you, man?"

The screaming stuttered, failed for a moment, and then began again. This time with words. "Balfour? Get out! Flee before they find you!"

A chill raced down Balfour's spine, and he hesitated between moving toward the man's voice and heeding his warning. With a growl, he turned back, running hunched almost double in the direction of the rope, shaft, and life.

The filthy earth squelched under his feet. And under other feet as well. Where Winters' voice had competed only with silence before, now there was a scuttling as of a million rats. Balfour steadied his grip on the blade.

The five things that blocked his path were not rats. The beasts stood on four legs, the size of hunting dogs with powerful haunches and thin, mobile forelegs. Their pale skins sported scaberous black growths like great, rough scales of a terrible insect. Great jaws hung open, teeth set on the exterior of lipless mouths. Their eyes were massive and black as wet coal, and they held a terrible and alien intelligence. As Balfour stood, waiting to see whether the beasts would attack, the nearest of them chittered, its voice high and cruel and articulated in fashion that carried the impression of speech without the meaning. More inhuman voices came from the deeper darkness. These were the vanguard of some greater force, and Balfour had the sickening certainty that the host was vast.

One of the beasts on Balfour's left darted forward too quickly for the eye to see. Long-honed reflex brought Balfour's blade to his defense, but the attack had been a mere feint. The beast jumped back, and two on the right leapt in toward him. He fell back, swinging his razor-sharp blade. The dog-like beasts retreated, but not so far as they had been. Balfour knew he was being driven back, but the knowledge redeemed nothing. He was on their territory, encumbered by the weight of stone and earth above him as well as the desperate need to protect the dim and flickering light in his off hand.

Inch by inch, foot by foot, they pressed him into the darkness. Twice, the animals came too near and Balfour's blade drew forth a yelp of pain and a thick black ichor. Once, his reaction came too slowly, and one of the dagger-like exposed teeth scraped against his shin, coming away pink with his blood. The passage began to slope down behind him, giving the beasts the high ground. He sensed the drop off as a change in the sound behind him. There was neither choice nor hope. He leapt back into the abyss without taking his eyes from his attackers.

His feet struck wet ground not more than six feet from the drop-off's lip. The beasts chittered among themselves and then fell back into the blackness.

The cell, for there was no other interpretation, was little more than a pit ten paces across. The man who squatted at its far edge had once been Daniel Winters. His skin was pale now, his hair and beard thick with the gray mud. An angry wound stood half-healed across his ribs and welts marked his arms, feet, and throat. An old scar split the back of a filthy hand.

"Well, old man," Winters said, his voice hoarse and pained, "Sorry to see you here."

"Sorry to've come," Balfour said. "Thought I was rescuing you."

"Appears I was bait," the thin man said with a shrug. "I thought the bastards were tormenting me for the joy of it, or I'd have warned you sooner. They do that sometimes.

Torture me for pleasure. And Christ alone knows what they've been giving me as food."

"What are they?"

"Lords of the underworld," Winters said. "Kings of a dark empire that spans half a continent."

"Mm."

Balfour eyed the wall of slick clay at the pit's edge. Scrambling up it might be possible if one of them gave the other a leg up. At a guess, they were no more than thirty yards from rope and shaft. Near enough that a tortured man's cries might reach the surface and call down help that could itself be captured.

"I think they won't return so long as the lantern holds," Winters said. "They've no love of light. They can stand it, but it hurts them. I don't suppose you've brought Meriwether with you as well?"

"He'll be along."

"How soon?"

Balfour considered. The prospects of a good outcome seemed dim indeed. He placed the lamp gently onto the ground, stepped back, and lifted his wide hands to his mouth in a rough speaking trumpet.

"Don't come down!" Balfour bellowed. "It's a trap! Don't come down!"

"He's up there, then?"

"Will be eventually," Balfour said, and resumed his deep-throated bellow, "Meriwether! Don't come down!"

Winters' chuckle was devoid of anything like real mirth. "How long do you think you can keep that up, old man?"

"Lifetime, I suppose," Balfour said.

❧

MERIWETHER SQUATTED at the edge of the pit, his face set in a scowl. The toes of his boots hung out over the void, his greatcoat spread about him like an emperor's robes, and his paired pistols weighted his hands. The evening sun bloodied the shafts of light, turning the decrepit barn into something more like a slaughterhouse. He had spent the greater part of the afternoon tracing Balfour's steps. With each hour, the dread in his heart had grown. When the trail had led to the abandoned farmhouse, he recognized it at once as the structure from Michael Caster's nightmares. Balfour had traced the evil of Harrowmoor to its roots too quickly, and so Meriwether's warning was come too late.

"Don't come down! It's a trap!"

Years of musical training had sharpened his auditory awareness. He could hear in the echoes at the edges of the words how the stone shaft was acting like a speaker's trumpet, making the captive man seem nearer than he was. Even knowing it was an illusion, Meriwether felt himself pulled forward as if Balfour's rescue lay only just beyond the darkness, and by reaching out, he could retrieve him.

"D'ya hear me? *Don't come down!*"

Frustration bared Meriwether's teeth. Caster's voice spoke in his memory. *Very little which falls into that dark pit returns again to the light.* He rose with a growl and stalked back to the front of the farmhouse where his hired horse stood. He returned his pistols to their holsters only when he required free hands to take the reins.

The animal shifted under him as Meriwether mounted, aware of the violence of his emotions. He set his back to the sun and put heels to the poor beast's flanks. Their paired shadow stretched out before them, growing first longer and then fading as the land traded the red of sunset for twilight gray. Eerie lights shone in the deepening gloom, but the will-o-the-wisps found no audience in Meriwether. His attention was focused, and no force on earth or in heaven could sway it, and yet his mind was in riot. The image of Balfour beset by the unholy beasts of the underworld plucked at him, and with it a cold clay of unformed emotion that would in time become the relief of saving his old friend or the rage of avenging him. With clenched teeth, he tried to imagine what business Lord Carmichael might have had that had led them all to this, but there were no answers to be had. The miles passed at a gallop and too slowly. The silver crescent of the moon and wide spill of stars filled the sky before Meriwether reached his destination.

The sanitarium at night was if anything more forbidding than it had been in daylight. The white of the walls had a sepulchral appearance, and the single lantern that glimmered in a high, lonesome window looked like nothing so much as a candle lit in prayer or remembrance. Meriwether threw himself from the saddle and strode to the shut doors. He pounded for what seemed hours before he heard the bolt pulled back. The man standing before him wore an orderly's uniform and an annoyed expression.

"Help you, sir?"

"My name is Meriwether. I am acting in the name of the Queen. I must see Michael Caster immediately."

"I'm sorry, sir, but there are no visitors after sundown," the orderly said as he began to close the door. "Many of the patients are quite delicate, you see. Can't disturb their rest. If you'd be so kind as to come back in the morning, sir, we can—"

His voice trailed off and his face grew pale. His gaze was locked on the barrel of Meriwether's pistol some few inches from his eye. Meriwether's smile cracked like ice on a winter wave.

"I'm afraid I must insist," he said.

Nightfall had given the interior corridors of the sanitarium a funereal aspect. Shadows clung to the archways above them. The bubbling of the gaslights competed with exhausted coughing and occasional shrieks of pain. The close, warm air was acrid with the scent of medicinal herbs burned to keep the foul night air at bay. It occurred to Meriwether not for the first time that Harrowmoor Sanitarium was both a place of healing and an anteroom to the grave. The men who walked these halls or were wheeled down them, who lay in the beds and sat in the spring sun, were expected to die here. The orderly reached Caster's cell, withdrew a ring of bronze keys from his pocket, and undid the bolt. Meriwether took the key from him, the pistol never straying from the white-shirted man's temple.

"My thanks," Meriwether said. "You may go. By all means inform the chief physician that I've returned and that I was unwilling to be put off."

"Y-yes, sir."

Meriwether holstered the pistol and lifted an eyebrow. The orderly moved away, one slow step at a time, and then a trot, and then a run. The footsteps receded. Meriwether didn't know whether there would be some consequence of his well-armed rudeness, and futhermore, he didn't greatly care. He rapped smartly on Caster's cell door, then pushed it open.

Caster sat at his desk. He still wore his trousers from earlier in the day, but had removed his shirt. The solidity of his physique spoke to hours spent in vigorous effort, even in this hopeless oubliette by the sea. He held a pen in one hand and a notebook lay flat on the table before him. He glanced up at Meriwether with a mixture of surprise and anger. The thumb-thick stub of candle cast deep shadows across his cheek.

"Mr. Meriwether," Caster said. "I am surprised. Have you thought of some other insult or cruelty since this morning?"

"There is need of you, sir. My colleague Mr. Balfour has discovered the unholy well you saw in your dreams. He has entered it, I believe in pursuit of Mr. Winters, with the result that he is now trapped underground and at the mercy of the beasts you have drawn in your books. It is my intention to retrieve them both. You are in sufficient health, you are accustomed to the rigors of violence, and you have the nearest thing to direct experience of the tunnels and their ungodly inhabitants. Circumstances being as they are, you are required."

Caster's laughter was vinegar and ashes. "Do you not see where I am, sir? I have served the crown as well as any man living. I have made my obeisance before God's altar. Men who have done less than I are hailed as heroes, and I am sent to this prison-in-all-but-name. Without even the dignity of a trial, I have been sentenced. This room you see before you will be my residence until I contract a fever from some other inmate here, and then they will bury me on the moor. Do you deny any of this?"

"I do not."

"Then by what satanic pride do you bring yourself to ask me for help? Or have you reconsidered your opinion? Now that I am of use, have I become less a monster?"

Meriwether took a deep breath and squared his shoulders. "Your nature has not changed, nor my opinion of it. It would be disingenuous of either of us to pretend otherwise. That is not the issue at hand."

"You think not? It seems very much so to me."

From behind him, Meriwether heard the sounds of voices lifted in alarm. He took no notice of them. "It is not a moral failure of the tiger that it was born a killer of men. But that it did not choose means nothing. Even if the tiger wished to be gentle, we cannot treat it as if it were a lamb. What you are, you are, and it bears no significance in this. Were you a murderer or a rapist or a saint, it would make no change to the situation of Balfour or Winters. It would neither add a single beast to the dark places underground nor subtract one. What must be done remains the same."

"Except that you are asking me to do it."

The voices came closer. Meriwether's pale gaze locked on Caster's. The candle flame spat, shuddered and then stood straight. Without looking away, Meriwether drew his pistols. Caster's jaw slid forward in defiance. Meriwether shifted one of the weapons around, holding it out by its barrel. Only then did Caster glance down at it and then back. He made no move to accept it.

"I have not come to beg your aid. I am here to inform you that two men are at the mercy of those same beasts that have haunted your nightmares. I have done so. You now know this to be the case. It is your conscience, not me, who must be your guide from there."

Caster turned away, his shoulders shifting as he went back to his opened book. A monstrous hound looked up at him from the page, half drawn and demonic. Meriwether did not move, did not lower the weapon held out to the soldier, adventurer, explorer, and invert. In the corridor, someone yelped from quite nearby. Caster glanced back at him with tear-filled eyes.

"You are a bastard, sir," Caster said, his voice thick.

"I am also what I am," Meriwether said.

Caster rose, plucked a rough shirt from the bedside table and pulled it over his head. Now clothed, he took the proffered handgun.

"If it is of any comfort to you," Meriwether said, "I think there is no real virtue in serving only those who it is easy to serve. A man who loves only those who also love him has nothing in particular to recommend him."

"You may put the sentiment on my gravestone," Caster said, and a voice in the hallway called the charge. The orderly who had led Meriwether to the room and three more like him burst through the doorway. Meriwether spun, his foot catching the door even as it swung open, slamming it back and spoiling the assault. A tranquilizing rifle fired wildly and Caster and Meriwether lifted their guns. The men stopped, suddenly aware of their folly.

"Johnston," Caster said.

A moment later, the first of the orderlies realized that he was being addressed. He blinked at the men behind him, at Meriwether, and then his gaze shifted uncertainly to Caster. "S-sir?"

"Mr. Meriwether and I will require torches. And a great deal of rope."

CHAPTER THREE:

The Devil's Allies

AFTER LONG HOURS AND despite his best efforts, Balfour's voice roughened and failed. He tried pausing every few minutes and letting his throat rest. He tried singing. There was no water to slake his thirst, but he pressed on as long as he could. There was no way to know whether Meriwether had heard his shouted warnings, but neither was there a reason to save his efforts. A ruined throat now was the least of his troubles. The slick, glistening walls of the pit that he and Winters shared was likely climbable, but he had little doubt that the black-eyed beasts had set sentries nearby. Even had they been able to haul one another out of the hole, they would only have been driven back into it. Cheese in the mousetrap.

Winters sat on the ground beside the little lamp. He had turned the wick low until the flame was little more than a bright ember. Even to Balfour's dark-adapted eyes, the world had lost all color. All that remained was the gold of the light and the black of the grave.

At last, Balfour sat. The muddy clay made wet, unpleasant sounds under him. He considered Winters. Remnants of the vital, bawdy, violent man still clung to his wasted frame. The bright, intelligent eyes were dull from exhaustion, starvation, and pain. The mud that caked Winters made him seem almost one with the walls and floor. As if the tunnels were absorbing him directly.

"Well, you held out longer than I'd expected," Winters said.

"Same of you," Balfour croaked.

Winters managed a smile. "They'll come back, you know. As soon as this little glimmer you've brought dies, they'll come back. And we'll wish they hadn't. Don't suppose you've learnt that Jewish trick?"

"Jewish trick?"

"Because if you could make this oil last a full eight days, I would very much appreciate it."

The man was on the edge of babbling. Winters' growing fear was as unnerving as the beasts themselves. Balfour drew one of his blades and began cleaning his nails. There was hardly more than a smear of oil remaining in the little lamp, but it was a small thing. He tried to guess how many hours he had been down in the darkness. Less than a full day, certainly. But time had become a curious thing, and somewhere in the adventure he'd managed to misplace his watch.

"More interesting than the usual blue rose affair," Balfour said.

"Blue rose? God. Did Carmichael tell you it was one of those? Cheeky bastard."

"Not what he told you?"

"He didn't need to tell me anything. I've known about these buggers far too long," Winters said, waiving an earth-colored hand toward the darkness at the top of the pit. "First time I've seen 'em with my own eyes, though."

"What are they? Demons?"

"No, old man. Not every devil's bargain is with the devil. They're animals just as we are, only we grew in the light and they the darkness. They live in the empty places of the earth, and nothing sane survives where they make their nests. We first made contact almost a century ago, but ever since the liberals kicked Disraeli out, they've been getting restless. Suppose they don't have much use for Gladstone. "

Balfour raised his eyebrows.

"It's true," Winters said. "Not supposed to talk about it, of course, but I can't see that it matters now. They're Britain's greatest and most secret allies. I know of two instances myself when the damned underminers saved us from ruin. They help us on the surface and we support them in their wars below. Munitions, labor, intelligence. All the requirements of war, whether you fight under the sky or under the ground. They aren't much for industry, and they like metal-works. I've seen the clock they built under Bucharest. Eerie damned thing. Carmichael's never trusted them, though. And he was right, he was right."

Balfour scowled at his blade weighing the new information passionlessly and waiting for Winters to go on. The Prime Minister was in league with fiends from beneath the earth and perhaps had been as long back as Pitt the Younger. Plausible enough. Winters coughed out a despairing laugh. Tears tracked down his filthy cheeks, but the tone of his words remained conversational as if they were talking business at the pub.

"All of this? It's a foothold. The first open betrayal. The agreement was always that they abandon their old centers here. They could tunnel under the continent until the whole thing was pocked as Swiss cheese, but the land under England was to remain inviolate. Only they've come back. When that poet fellow started reporting on them in his little sonnets, Carmichael and his crowd started spinning like tops. Sent me out to see if there was anything to it."

"Is," Balfour said.

"Yes. They've come where they swore they would not, and it's poisoned the land from bone to bird's nest. We should have burned them all out years ago, but there was always advantage to waiting just a bit longer," Winters said, then laughed. "Women or politics, this is always the hardest part of an alliance, isn't it?"

"What part?"

"The ending of it."

The wick dimmed, the light fading away to a low, red glow less than the tip of a lit cigar. Winters scrabbled at the lamp, drawing a fraction of an inch of wick up. There was nothing to burn now but the oil-soaked cotton itself. And when that was done, darkness. A scrabbling sound came from the edge of the pit, and for a moment, Balfour saw the huge, black eyes of one of their captors looking down at him. He flicked his wrist, the blade flying through the air. The dog screamed and retreated. Winters' chuckle was bleak and joyless.

"They'll make you pay for that, old friend."

"I'll make the trade."

"I suppose you will. Still, I was wondering if you'd be kind enough to break my neck for me when the lantern fails. I'd count it a kindness."

Balfour drew another blade and tried to decide whether Winters was in earnest. The filthy man's smile was weary. The wounds covered by the grime were too numerous to count.

"If you'd like," Balfour said.

A volley of animal screams rolled through the darkness, each one rising above the rest in an unholy chorus. Under the layer of mud, Winters' face paled. Balfour rose to his feet, flexing his shoulders and tossing the blade dexterously from one hand to the other. His gaze flicked from one side of the great pit to the other in silent anticipation. Winters stood as well, his body hunched over the dying lantern as if there might be some safety in it. Balfour paced.

"They're coming," Winters said.

"If they were coming, they'd be here," Balfour said. "Keep quiet."

Balfour closed his eyes, ignoring what little light remained. He strained his senses. The howl of the dogs, broken as it was into the gurgles and chirrups of unknown words. The slightest of breezes, barely a stirring in the air. And a scent so faint as to be almost hidden by the stink of the tunnels. Faint, but present and unmistakable. Burning pitch. And then the sharp sound of a pistol. Balfour grinned and opened his eyes.

"Bad news, Winters. Have to kill you some other time," he said, drawing a fresh blade and tossing it to the man. "We aren't dying today unless we get sloppy. Then, maybe."

"What are you saying?"

"The mad bastard never could take orders from me," Balfour said. "Point of pride or some such. Meriwether! Here! We're here in a damned pit! *Meriwether!*"

꧁꧂

THE MOON had set by the time Meriwether and Caster returned to the dead farmhouse and its gate to the underworld, but even by starlight, Meriwether had seen the unease growing in the set of his companion's shoulders and heard it in the tone of his voice. For him, they were quite literally riding into nightmare. Finding the barn had been short work, as had fixing the new length of rope beside the old. The two men worked in near silence. Balfour's voice no longer rang from the depths of the earth, but Meriwether assured himself that after so many hours, the silence was to be expected.

"The hounds will be watching for us, I expect," Caster said. "Even now, I imagine they can scent us."

"Then there is no call for us to be subtle," Meriwether said.

They descended together, Meriwether letting himself down hand over hand on the old, rough rope, Caster sliding down the newer. Each carried half a dozen pitch-dipped torches, a small lantern, and one of Meriwether's pistols. There had been no time to gather more.

The descent took longer then Meriwether had anticipated, until it seemed as though earth and heaven had both disappeared. All that remained was the eternal stone, the abrading rope, and the rough breathing of the other man beside him. Time seemed to fade, leaving only the sense of urgency and the ache of physical effort. It was Caster who called the halt, his hand to Meriwether's shoulder. He struck a match, lighting one of the small torches. After the utter dark, the flame was painful and blinding. When Caster dropped it, it spiraled down fifteen, twenty, thirty feet, and then landed in soft muck. From the edge of the light, a dozen huge black eyes stared up at them and num-berless teeth chittered in anticipation. The smoke from the torch rose past them, stinking and warm.

"Well," Caster said. "It's what we came here for."

As one, the two men drew their pistols and began fir-ing down into the waiting enemy as they let the rope slide around their belaying grips. The beasts at the well's bottom scattered, their motions too fast for the eye to follow. The high, terrible voices rose together in panic or in threat. It reminded Meriwether of nothing so much as the cry that certain African insects made when some member of the hive has detected fire. When, moments later, the two men reached the well's base, Caster scooped up the guttering torch, lighting a second from its flame while Meriwether reloaded, then handed the torches over while he replen-ished his own ammunition. Two tunnels ran from the small chamber, and if Balfour had left any mark of his passage, the beasts had cleaned it away. The cacophony of bestial voices deafened.

From one of the tunnels, two beasts leapt. Their dagger teeth snapped at the air as Caster fired at first one then the other. Meriwether wheeled to the second opening, firing into the darkness and scattering the half dozen animals that had been preparing to attack from the flank.

"Bullets will serve us only so well," Caster shouted. "We must use flame."

"Not a great deal of free air down here," Meriwether said.

"Then we must use it efficiently." The poet's mad grin called forth its twin from Meriwether. "Which way?"

Meriwether paused. The chittering and screaming of the enemy poured forth from both tunnels, but there, hidden among them, the rolling bass of a familiar voice. *Damned pit. Meriwether!* Caster stuck one of the torches firmly in the mud to keep the pitch above the dampness, and together they pressed forward. The tunnel appeared empty, and they moved swiftly down its curving path. A soft skittering sound like a pebble rolling down a hillside cut through the noise.

"The walls, Caster! They're in the—"

The tunnel wall beside them collapsed, the rotten stone sloughing into gravel, and the battle was joined in earnest. Pale skin encrusted with black and scaberous growths pressed in against them. Teeth snapped. Meriwether felt a shudder of ripping cloth as his greatcoat suffered under some unseen tooth or claw. The quarters were too close, and his martial practice had not assumed so low an opponent. Meriwether was borne down by the sheer weight of alien flesh, his arms pulled to the sides by cruel teeth. Something struck the back of his head, and the world rang. The killing shrieks grew distant and muffled. A bright pain lit his ribs, and then the warm wetness of his own blood. A sense of terrible peace began to sweep over him.

Between one breath and the next, all around him turned to fire. The howls of the beasts took a different tone and his arms were his own again. A pistol fired very nearby, and for a moment he thought he had pulled the trigger himself. Caster was at his side, dragging him forward, and the tunnel behind them was awash in flames. One of the little lamps they'd carried down lay shattered in the center of the conflagration. The ambush had widened the tunnel, and tiny pools of flame marked the footsteps where one particularly unlucky dog had fled.

"Move quickly. There won't be air enough to breathe soon."

Meriwether nodded, and together the two men crawled on. The clay stank, the smoke stank. Hellish light flickered behind them, driving back the enemy and threatening them both with another manner of death. Balfour's hearty bellow was closer now. Two of the enemy beasts stood between them and the pit from whence the familiar voice arose. Meriwether shot them both.

The pit stood just deeper than a man, and it took Caster and Meriwether working as one and Winters lifting from below to pull Balfour to its lip, and then the concerted effort of the three men above to haul Winters to join them. Balfour's voice was rough from shouting, but he seemed none the worse for his captivity. Meriwether was shocked by Winters' diminished frame and barbaric appearance, but he said nothing. There was no time.

"We have to get back to the ropes," Meriwether said.

"Isn't far," Balfour said.

"We can't go back the way we came."

"Why not?"

"Caster set it on fire. If the flames have died by now, it's because they've run out of air."

"We can't stay here, men," Winters said, his voice trembling. "They'll reform their ranks. Likely they're coming already."

"You're bleeding," Balfour said.

"I'm aware of it," Meriwether said. "It is not my most pressing problem."

"Fair enough. But if our plan is to stumble upon some other way through dumb luck and—"

"I can get us there," Caster said. "I know these caves, and I can find the path back."

Balfour stroked his mustache. "How is it you know them?"

"I have been here many times in dreams," Caster said, his voice solemn. "And to trust in me is your only choice."

A howling rose from deep in the earth. An angry and martial noise, as unlike the previous cacophony as the first notes of a symphony from a drunken beer house chorus. Winters wept and bit his lips to keep from bawling. Balfour nodded to Caster.

"Lead on, then."

They portioned out the remaining torches so that each man carried fire in one hand and a weapon in the other. Caster and Balfour led the way, knife and pistol at the ready. Meriwether and Winters came behind. All held the flame toward the group's center as if protecting it, though in truth it was to keep from being blinded by the bare flame. The black tunnels twisted, rose, and fell like the arteries of a massive corpse. Smoke thickened the air, but there was no light apart from that which they carried. At each intersection, Caster would pause, look first down one tunnel and then the next, his brow set in terrible concentration. Once he had made a decision, he did not falter. Each man knew that their fate rested entirely upon Caster's judgment.

They reached a complex where three tunnels came together, creating a wide, rough chamber tall enough to stand upright. For a moment, they were silent, listening to the voices of their enemies.

"Coming from that way," Balfour said, gesturing with a bare blade to the narrowest of the passages.

"And yet, that is where we must go," Caster answered.

Winters' mouth went hard and his eyes shifted anxiously. "No room to fight. Not enough air for four torches and eight lungs either, I'd wager you. Let's try out the other ways first."

Balfour turned back to Meriwether, eyebrows lifted in query. Meriwether's wry smile was answer enough. Together, they moved toward the narrow passage.

"Are you mad, then?" Winters said. "That's death. I'm not going that way."

"Your choice," Balfour said, and they set off, Winters muttering angrily at the rear.

The walls pressed and the ceiling lowered, the flames from the torches licked the stone above them and stained it with soot. When it became impossible to walk abreast, Balfour doused his torch in the muck, pulled a second blade, and took the lead alone without discussion. Meriwether kept close at his back with light and pistol, ready to fire past his compatriot's shoulder should the occasion come. They moved forward with the speed and efficiency of long acquaintance. The passageway dipped, passing through a puddle of foul sludge, and then rose again, narrowing further. With every step, the voices of the enemy grew louder and the air they breathed, thicker and more oppressive.

"Balfour," Meriwether said. "The torch."

Balfour looked back. The flame in Meriwether's hand danced and undulated, but Balfour saw it too. Without sheathing his blade, he licked a fingertip and held it out before them.

"What's the matter? Why've we stopped?" Winters hissed.

"Fresh breeze," Balfour said. "We're almost there, boys."

"Though this last may be the least pleasant," Meriwether said.

Five yards ahead, the tunnel turned sharply to the left. As they approached it, the chittering and howls rose. With a sigh, Balfour knelt and scooped up a thin handful of the thick clay over which they walked. Meriwether turned back to the men behind him. "Dreadfully sorry about this, but we poor Hades-bound brothers of Ulysses have no wax to spare."

"What?" Winters said.

"Use the muck to stop up your ears," Caster said.

"This may be loud," Meriwether said.

With a shout, Balfour charged the little turning, Meriwether as close behind him as he could manage. A dozen dogs blocked the way, teeth and claws clacking, but none so fiercely as Balfour's blades. As he pushed back the press of the enemy with the combination of blade, brute strength, and bloodthirst, Meriwether strode behind, firing bullet after bullet with an air of calm and calculation. Each pull of the trigger accounted for one enemy's life. When the pistol went dry, Caster plucked it from Meriwether's hand and slapped a freshly loaded pistol in its place. Foot by foot, they pushed back the horde, walking over the dead and dying alike. The beasts broke and ran just as they passed through an archway of stone and found themselves again at the base of the great shaft, the two ropes waiting where they had been.

"I'm bit," Winters said as he stumbled out, his torch held high above him. "One of the little bastards wasn't dead. Took a chunk out of my ankle."

"Can you walk?" Meriwether asked.

"If it means leaving here, I'll take it off at the knee and run on the stump."

"Up, then," Balfour said, handing Winters the thinner and newer of the ropes. "I'll follow close."

"In case I fall?"

"Can't have you landing on their heads," Balfour said, then turned to Meriwether. "Hold the ground?"

"We will not lose an inch of it, though the demons of hell rise up for it. Will we, Mr. Caster?"

"Same as any war, we'll win so long as the ammunition holds."

Winters and Balfour put hand to the ropes, and rose up into the black. Neither man had a hand to spare, so Winters strapped the second lantern to his belt. In surprisingly little time, the light grew tiny above them, no brighter than a weak, flickering star. Meriwether reloaded the pistols as Caster lit the last of the torches, throwing all but one down the tunnels to discourage another wave of attack.

"You did well," Meriwether said.

"I'm a soldier," Caster said.

"More than that," Meriwether said. "You're a man with a useful parlor trick."

The minutes stretched out like hours, days, eons. The voices of the dogs returned once, but the beasts did not brave the light. Almost imperceptibly, a new noise rose: a roaring as of a great fire a long way off. The torches fluttered under a new and noxious breeze, one that stank of fish and rot and cold.

"What's that, do you think?" Caster asked.

"Hoping not to find out," Meriwether said.

At last, Balfour's voice came from some unseeable heaven above them. "Lines are clear. Tie on, and we'll pull you up."

Caster and Meriwether lost no time, wrapping the ropes around their waists and fastening knots. The foul breeze was faster now, moving out from both of the tunnels. The torches guttered, their flames growing low and dim. The roaring was perceptibly louder now.

"Pull, man!" Meriwether called. "They've called up the Devil."

The roar grew suddenly louder. Meriwether felt a terrible intent in the sound, as if the earth itself were bent on his murder. In the dim and failing light, Caster's face was pale and fearful. As was his own. Between one breath and the next, the ropes dug into them, and they rose up through the shaft, faster than any human strength could have taken them. Meriwether looked down to see the tunnels below them burst open and a great, grayish flesh overcome the tiny torches. He had the impression, in that last momentary illumination, of a single vast body, crushing the ground itself. He fired down, Caster following his lead, and then they were in darkness. Only the muzzle flash showed the rising tide of ropy grey, climbing up the shaft faster than any man could, but not so quickly as Caster and Meriwether were pulled.

At the mouth of the well, Balfour took their shoulders and hauled them up. The ropes, once tied to the structure of the barn, now led out through its ruined doors into the pale

blue of the coming dawn. Meriwether turned at the stone's edge to look back, half expecting to see the monstrosity clawing its way up after them, flowing up from the poisoned earth like a geyser. But the threat of daylight appeared to hold this new evil at bay. He let himself breathe a shuddering sigh of relief.

"Reinforcements?" Balfour said.

"Apparently our demonic hounds aren't the only danger in this buried and bestial England," Meriwether said. "Still, so long as light is our ally, we have hope."

"Light and black powder," Balfour said.

"Yes," Meriwether agreed. "A very great deal of black powder. And before sundown tonight. That may take some doing."

"Horses," Caster said, a chuckle in his voice. Balfour and Meriwether turned to consider him. The man leaned against the wall of the ruined barn, his face and shirt streaked with muck. A deep scratch marked his shoulder, the flesh proud and pink, but not bloody. "You used the horses to pull us up."

"Winters' idea," Balfour said.

"And likely our salvation," Meriwether said. "How dire are his wounds?"

"Bite's bad," Balfour said. "And he's been tormented for some time. Weakened him."

Meriwether nodded. His gaze returned to the black well and its ancient stone. "He must take one horse and you

the other. If anyone can convince Lord Carmichael of the gravity of the situation, it will be him. There is a telegraph station in Harrowmoor. You must see him safely there."

"And you?" Balfour asked, stroking his mud-caked mustache.

"Caster and I will remain here and see that nothing from below chooses to brave the light."

Invisible in the gloom of the barn, the sun rose over the moors of England, and rays of bright gold shot through the holes and broken slats of the barn like a host of angels. Caster looked up, exhausted and smiling. Balfour caught Meriwether's gaze and nodded once at Caster in mute query. Meriwether's smile was reassurance enough.

"We'll be back by midday," Balfour said.

"We will await your return," Meriwether said.

Balfour nodded once and stepped out the doors. The sound of his gruff, low voice still hoarse from shouting mixed with the half-laughing, half-weeping Winters. Meriwether squatted against the wall, letting the ruined wood support him. The pain of his injuries made themselves known, but not with such urgency that they could not still be ignored. His nose, inured now to the vicious stink of the underworld, could only find the scents of heather and dew. Caster's eyes were fixed on the well, his expression a mixture of loathing and longing. Hoof beats retreated into the quiet English morning. Meriwether waited until they were gone entirely before he broke the silence.

"Not, I suppose, the evening you had expected."

"No, not at all," Caster said. "Nor the morning, for that matter. Just now I'd normally be eating thin oatmeal and a particularly vile sort of apple butter that the cooks seem to think stimulating to the bowels. Instead, I'm here, half dead from exhaustion and hunger, and with no particular expectation of food or water for hours yet."

"I appreciate your sacrifice."

"I haven't made one," Caster said, his voice throbbing with a desperate passion. "I'd have chosen this a thousand times over. I was a soldier once. I have slept naked under the stars of Africa. I have watched lions stalk me and my party. I have carried a man I loved more than life itself bleeding through a battlefield. Dying by inches in my own private Elba, waiting for consumption to consume me? It isn't a fate I'd wish on a dog."

"I appreciate that as well," Meriwether said.

They were silent for a long moment. The light that spilled through the air seemed not to dispel the darkness. Caster shifted, stood. For all their trials and troubles, his frame was straight, his shoulders unbowed. The expression on his face was sour, and he gripped Meriwether's pistol in his fist. Meriwether stood as well and took a step toward the man. When Caster spoke, his voice held disgust, fascination, and a firmness of resolve.

"I find myself acutely aware of being outside the sanitarium, armed, and with only one man to guard me. I think it might be best for us both if I returned this to you, sir."

A smile plucked at Meriwether's lips and he drew his wallet from the pocket of his coat. "Best that you keep it, I think. You may have need of it, and it's better to have it and not want it than the reverse." He tossed the leather across the space. It caught the light like a pigeon's wings. Caster caught it with his off hand, but his eyes were on Meriwether. "I will tell them that there was an attack from below," Meriwether said. "That you were taken. When they disbelieve me, I will admit that you became distraught at the prospect of returning to your rest cure and leapt to your death below. They will have no reason to disbelieve me twice."

"Ah," Caster said. "I've become an acceptable monstrosity, have I? Made all the right steps, and now I'll be permitted to slink off under some assumed name. I have no illusions about your opinion of me, sir. Or your judgment of what I am."

Rather than explain, Meriwether crossed the space between them in two fast strides, the force of his movement carrying him into the other man's body like a blow. One hand took Caster's hip as if to throw him, but only lifted him off his balance. His other arm locked around the back of Caster's neck, constraining and cradling his head in the same movement. Caster's lips against his own were sweet and strong. The stubble where the man had not shaved scratched against him. For a moment, Caster was frozen, and then, slowly, his mouth moved in answer. Meriwether savored the moment, locking it in the vault of his memory. The warmth of the man's body, the taste of his mouth. All of it precious as gold.

He gave Caster back his balance and stepped away. When he spoke, Meriwether's voice was thick with desire and regret. "Go to the continent. To Paris. Montmartre. There is a man named Andreas Croft. A painter and a poet. He will help you."

Caster began to speak, failed.

Meriwether went on. "When you find him, tell him… tell him Alexander sends his love."

Caster stood stunned for a moment, then bowed, a brief gesture as a schoolboy might make to a tutor. When he stepped out into the bright morning light, his expression was complex and vivid. Joy and sorrow, determination and gratitude and pity. Or perhaps Meriwether only imagined those things. It was hard to be certain. The footsteps grew faint much more quickly than the hoof beats had, and Meriwether waited longer after they had vanished to step out to the sunlight himself and await the return of his colleagues and compatriots and enough black powder, he hoped, to seal the well forever.

"I AM sorry as hell, boys," Lord Carmichael said. Outside the windows of the King Street flat, April was giving way to May. A gentle rain fell from sun-bright skies and scented the earth with its passage. "I wanted to tell you what you were heading into, but the Prime Minister expressly forbade it."

"In fairness, you did hint rather broadly that there was more to the situation than met the eye," Meriwether said.

Lord Carmichael smiled. "Well, the PM didn't expressly forbid that, now did he?"

The flat stood in disarray around them. Balfour's notebooks lay open on the desk to a page illustrating an obscure mechanism of war inspired by Da Vinci. Meriwether's disassembled pistols covered a drop cloth before the mantle, awaiting some new modification. Inexplicably, a small grey kitten dozed undisturbed on the ottoman beside Balfour's booted feet, its nose tucked beneath its tail. Lord Carmichael stood before the window, watching as the tiny raindrops streaked the glazing. Horseshoes and cartwheels clattered across the cobblestones.

The battle of Harrowmoor had lasted two days while Lord Carmichael and his circle in government descended upon the abandoned farmhouse and all that lay beneath it. The victory had been hard-won but decisive, and returning to the more familiar world of London was like returning from foreign wars.

"I continue to marvel at the thought that those rude beasts were once allies of the crown," Meriwether said.

"It's the business of empire," Lord Carmichael said with a shrug. "We make alliances with the ungodly and unsavory when we must. They aren't marriages. When the world changes, we can free ourselves of them. We found these subterranean bastards, and they were of use to us as we were to them. It doesn't matter to us what ungodly horror lives in a cave three miles below daylight. One's as good as another to me. But tunnels dug wherever we want? Battlements undermined without the loss of a single soldier? Those were as good as gold."

"They're devils," Balfour said.

"Alas, they aren't," Lord Carmichael said. "Had one meet with the archbishop. No fear of the cross, no discomfort with holy water. But, in truth, I can't say we'd have shied away from the devil, if he'd been able to assure the stability and greatness of England. It's an ugly truth, and we don't proclaim it from the rooftops, but in governance, expedience often wins over principle. We allied ourselves with the hounds because if we didn't, the Russians might. And we stood by each other until we didn't, and now we'll do everything we can to destroy them."

"And what of loyalty?" Meriwether said. "Last I checked it was still among the virtues."

"Are you serious?" Lord Carmichael asked. "You can't be loyal to something like *that*."

"Well," Meriwether said with a grin, "at least we can enjoy our return to righteousness and the side of angels."

"And thank God for it," Lord Carmichael said. "Those damned things made my flesh crawl. I'm much happier working to kill them than fighting at their sides. It will be a long campaign, though. And fought for the most part in secrecy and silence. We'll prevail with time, though. Count on that."

The kitten woke, yawned, stretched and bounded off into the clutter as Lord Carmichael finished the last of his brandy.

"Well," he said, "I had best be off. Have to go see Winters in hospital. You heard that bite of his has gone septic?"

"Hadn't," Balfour said.

"May need to have the leg off," Lord Carmichael said, rising to his feet. "It's a damned shame. Those abominable things are rife with disease. World will be better off without 'em."

As his carriage pulled into the street traffic, Meriwether looked down through the window. The sidewalks were filled with the business of humanity, men and women passing each other on their ways to whatever errands the day demanded of them. Umbrellas had bloomed like morning glories at dawn. Balfour rose to his feet with a grunt.

"You notice he made no mention of Caster," Meriwether said.

"The pervert? Why should he?"

"He saved us."

"So did the horses. Carmichael didn't talk of them either. Caster was a troubled man, and now he's a dead one. Blessing for him that he died in a good cause."

"I suppose."

Balfour trundled to the desk, drew a pencil from the drawer, and addressed himself to the diagrams. For some minutes, the only sound in the flat was of the sharpened lead scratching the paper.

"Something bothering you?" Balfour asked without looking over.

"Idle thoughts," Meriwether said. "Pointless speculations. The scattered leaves of a mind shedding itself like September oaks."

"Mm?"

"I was thinking what it would be to live one's whole life underground," Meriwether said, his voice mellowed by longing and sorrow. "To never see the sun or feel its warmth upon one's brow. Never to smell the rain. There is an entire civilization like that."

"Not a human one."

"No," Meriwether said, pulling the cord that would summon Mrs. Long. "Not a human one."

The housekeeper entered the room with a pot of tea and a plate of sandwiches. Meriwether stepped forward and plucked a teacup from under a stack of papers, then held it out to be filled. The scent of tea was like civilization.

"I don't believe I said it when you came, sir," Mrs. Long said, "but it is a pleasure to have you both back."

"And we are pleased to be here," Meriwether said. Balfour grunted his assent.

"How can I be of service, sir?" she asked.

"If you would be so kind, I believe it is time to send out for certain scientific supplies," Meriwether said.

Mrs. Long nodded knowingly. "You'll be wanting another pig, then."

JULIUS CAME again today, and brought his son with him. Little Alan will be eight this summer, and already there is a brilliance to his mind that I find astonishing. If he grows to fulfill the promise that shows in him now, he will be a force to be reckoned with. And yet, tonight, I find myself apprehensive.

It is not possible, is it, that I can detect a kindred soul at so young an age and unformed a character? And yet there is something about the boy that recalls certain men of my acquaintance as though it were a family resemblance. For his own sake, I pray that it is a misapprehension brought on by old age and infirmity. And yet, as the hour grows late, I fear for him.

God makes all things. The true and the twisted are likewise the work of His hand. It is my own will and the restraining hand of my fellows that has kept my base instincts and peculiarity from blooming out into sin. And so I may be permitted to hope that little Alan is spared this burden that I have carried, or that if it is his as well, that he contains it as I have or perhaps better. Otherwise I fear whatever he may accomplish in the world will be overshadowed, and his name recognized only for his failures.

History has no kindness for abominations.